DRINK IT DOWN

Curves Just Wanna Have Fun, book 4

MEGAN WADE

IMOGEN

Tap, tap, tap, the sound of knuckles knocking on my bedroom door. I sigh but say nothing.

"Come *onnn*, Imogen! It's practically *illegal* to skip out on Saint Paddy's day," my roommate and bestie, Riley, whines from outside my room. "How dare you resist the call of a lovely pint of Guinness and obnoxious dancing."

I roll my eyes from the edge of my bed, then glance longingly at my laptop. I'm totally not up for going out tonight, especially not to party with the masses. All I really want to do is curl up under my covers and binge Bridgerton for the fifth time. Step aside, McSteamy, the Duke has arrived!

Bump, bump, bump... Riley's palm slaps my door and takes me away from my fantasies before they can even begin. "Imogen Walsh!

I know you're in there and I know you're trying to ignore me, but I'm not gonna letcha!"

I hear the threatening sound of keys jingling, and I speedily pull a sweater over me before opening the door to a grinning Riley. "Why do I have to go, Riles? You know I have a job interview on Friday—a very *important* one, mind you—and if you haven't already noticed: it's Thursday! I don't want to be wiped out before it."

She pushes through and plops on the armchair in the corner of my room. "Thursday-schmursday! It's St. Patrick's Day today!" I open my mouth to retort, but she cuts me off. "Yes, yes, I'm aware you have that interview tomorrow. You've spoken about it constantly for a week. I'm not daft."

I lean against the door frame, cross my arms, and glare at her. "Then why are you forcing me to go out?"

She gasps and covers her mouth in false disbelief. "Me, being forceful? Why, I'd never do such a thing." She gets up from the chair and comes up to pull me into a hug. "I've not seen you all week with you going crazy preparing for this interview. I just want to bring you some good ol' Irish luck, and what better way to get it than from celebrating the patron saint of Ireland himself?"

"Fine." I hug her back. "I'll go."

She squeals and squeezes me tighter. "We'll go out for one drink, then I'll let you on your merry way to your beauty sleep, OK?"

"Only one?"

"Maybe three... Or four..."

"*Riley*."

She exhales an exaggerated sigh. "Fine, only one...for you." Then she goes off to my closet and rummages through. "Now, let's see here. What have you got that's green and sexy?"

I can only roll my eyes and sigh. She knows very well that 'sexy' isn't in my clothing vocabulary. I'm more of the comfy type, though that doesn't mean I don't like to dress up.

"Ach, gosh, Imogen, we really need to get you some new stuff." She grunts as she tosses item after item out of my closet.

I pick up a green V-neck short-sleeved dress—my favorite—and gasp. "What's wrong with this one?"

She glances up at me from my cupboard and cringes. "Lass, you've had that dress since we were in school."

I raise an eyebrow. "And?"

"And you *need new* clothes," she says in response before rummaging through my closet again. I mentally count the seconds with my arms crossed as Riley tosses my clothes on the floor. I count ninety items before she falls on her butt in a huff.

I grin. "Any luck?"

She glares at me from the floor. "You know very well the answer to that question."

I giggle, then pick up my favorite dress and get into it then and there. Standing in front of my standing mirror, I flatten the dress and whistle to myself. "Ya know, Riles, you can't beat a classic."

She flips me off with a kiss before heading to her room and getting herself ready. Chuckling to myself, I sit at my make-up desk and go for the minimal look. I'm not dressing to impress tonight—I'm literally having *one* drink, and then I'm coming straight back. I apply some eyeliner and mascara to my baby blues, some lipstick to my pouty lips, and give my reflection the nod of approval.

As I finish brushing my long, black hair, Riley knocks on my room's door frame. "Ready when you are, lass." She sighs. "Really, Imogen? At least put some eyeshadow on."

I take another glance at myself in the

mirror, and smile. "Nope, not tonight." I get up and brush past her.

"Fiiiiiiine," she huffs before meeting me by the front door. "And it pains me to admit it, but you do look mighty fine in that ancient dress of yours."

With a laugh, I open the door and stick the crook of my arm out to Riley. "And you always look stunning. Those blokes at the pub won't know what hit them once the two of us walk in there."

"Not that they'll have a chance with you since you're drinking one then leaving."

"That'll just mean there's more for you," I say with a giggle as we walk out of the apartment together, arm in arm, all the while knowing that as much as I say I'll only have one drink and go home, once I start having fun, I'll forget all about my interview and regret it in the morning.

LEO

I slide into the plush, bright green seat of our booth and glance around the Getting Lucky pub. It's homey. In the way that all traditional Irish pubs are with its exposed dark-wood interior. You'd think that a pub owned by a thirty-three-year-old would be 'new' in a way, but there are scuff marks within the planks of the floors that show the age of the place.

Finn and Conor, part of our landing party tonight, sit across from me while Sam, my business-partner-in-crime at Tru Blu Marketing, shuffles into the booth next to me. "What a sight, eh, mate?" His Aussie accent, twice the thickness of my own, is full of admiration. "I can't believe we managed to get a seat. This place is chokas!"

He's right, the pub is nearly packed full of Irishmen and non-Irishmen alike, flowing in and out of the few local pubs that this quaint little Irish village of Duthmoore has to offer, all to celebrate Saint Patrick's Day. I shrug. "Apparently, Conor's tight with the owner. He's that big, tattooed guy minding the bar."

"Ha! Anyone in Duthmoore's *tight* with our lad Cillian over there. Even Finn here. I'm just even tighter, being a cousin and all," Conor says as he laughs a jolly laugh, his bright blue eyes crinkling at the edges. The rest of us can't help but laugh along with him, his energy being so magnetic and positive. I've known Conor since we both went to university in London. When he heard that I was going to Belfast, he insisted that we spend St. Paddy's Day in his hometown.

So, here I am, in a random village in the north of Ireland, going to have a weekend out in my mate's family cottage. A weekend of drinking and hunting and being very manly—that was Conor's guarantee.

The sound of a chair being scraped across the floor brings the table's attention to Aidan, another one of our fine Irish hosts, tugging his chair at the side of the booth. "First round's on me, lads," he says as he sits down, earning cheers.

As if by clockwork, a waitress comes around with a tray of pints and expertly places each one on the table without dropping even a single dribble of foam. I read her name tag— Aoifa—and my Aussie brain has zero idea how to even begin to *try* to pronounce it. "Here's round one, lads," she says with a smile. A murmur of appreciation emanates from around the table.

Aidan, in his boyish demeanor, smiles at her. "Ah, cheers, Aoife. You're an absolute angel." He says her name as 'ee-fa', like a German saying 'Eva', except with an elongated 'e'. My mind hurts trying to understand the logic of Irish names. Aidan tries to place a hand on Aoife's arm, and she swiftly smacks it away with her tray. "Ow!" he yelps, earning roaring laughter from Conor and Finn.

"No touching what doesn't belong to ya," she says with a wink before leaving the table. She walks away with a slightly more pronounced sway to her hips, and all Aidan can do is stare after her, jaw wide open.

Conor pats Aidan on the shoulder. "Aw, cheer up, lad. At least now you know those boyish charms are no good for a fine lass like that." Aidan puts his face into his hands, earning another bellowing laugh from the other Irishmen. "To good ol' Saint Paddy!" he yells. We all bump our pint glasses and drink to the Irish patron saint.

"Oi, Aussies, what's that drinking song from Down Under? The one about the piss pot," Conor says, smacking his pint glass onto the tabletop, some of his Guinness splashing onto it and causing Aidan to yelp at the loss of good ale.

"Mate," I say, lengthening the word as I look over to Sam, who gives me a knowing look in return. If there's one thing that us Australians love, it's drinking and singing. He proceeds to crack his knuckles and looks at the Irishmen seriously.

"All right. We'll do that one. But I don't think you're ready for it," Sam says as he smacks my shoulder.

"Oh, yeah, you guys definitely aren't ready for it," I say as I resist the urge to grin. If there's anything the *Irish* live for, it's drinking and singing. We're baiting them, and we know it—a little friendly country to country rivalry.

Conor belts out a jolly laugh, which Aidan and Finn promptly join in. "You lot think you can out drink the Irish? Dream on!"

"We can, and we do," Sam says with a laugh. "The first thing the convicts did when they got off the boat was start stealing potatoes to make alcohol."

"You're talking about potatoes to the

Irish?" Conor says, almost crying with tears. "Just sing the bloody song, man. We're dehydrating just listening to ya."

I lose all composure and laugh along. "Well, all right then," I say as I push Sam's pint glass closer to him. "Wanna be the first cab off the rank?"

"Do I ever." Sam gives me a wink and readies himself with a pint glass in hand. "Ready when you are, mate."

I clear my throat and start. The others join in quickly as they remember the words from previous drinking sessions. "*Here's to Sam, he's true blue! He's a piss pot through and through. He's a bastard, so they say. He's meant to go to heaven, but he went the other way*"— Sam brings his glass to his lips before I finish —"*He's going down! Down! Down!*"— Sam starts to chug down his beer, and the Irishmen shout along with me—"*Down! Down! Dooooown!*"

Sam smacks his glass to the table when he's done, earning a round of hooting and cheering from the rest of us. "And that's how it's done Down Under!" he shouts. "Now, who's next?"

Finn pats Aidan on the back and belts out, "*Here's to Aidan, he's true blue!*" Aidan groans but picks up his glass as the rest of the table follows along. I quietly excuse myself from the table and head over to the bar.

"Hey, mate, could we get four more pints of Guinness plus a water?" I ask the gruff-looking bar-owner when I arrive at the bar.

"Sure." He grunts. "That'll be fifteen off of ya." I promptly pull out my wallet and hand him a twenty-pound note. He nods and starts pouring the pints.

"A bit old for the drinking games, aren't ya?" a female voice chirps from behind me.

"Hey, who you calling old?" I start to say as I turn around to meet the owner of the voice. I have to keep my jaw from dropping. *Wow...*

Leaning against the bar is someone I could only describe as an angel. Her long, straight black hair flows to the tops of her voluptuous breasts, which seem to be perfectly enhanced by the curves of the rest of her body. Her smiling lips are full and delicious, the color of wine, and a smile radiates within her striking blue eyes. A stiffness starts to form in my pants. She is absolutely *breathtaking*. I *want* her.

I clear my throat and regain my composure, leaning against the bar. "At what point is a man too old to have fun?" I remark, a smirk on my lips.

Her eyebrows raise, and her sapphire

eyes instantly light up. "Australian. Wouldn't have guessed. What in the world could bring your kind to Duthmoore of all places?"

"You know, I wasn't sure," I say, scratching my bearded chin before looking deep into her blue eyes, like two ocean pearls to drown in. "But now I'm thinking that maybe it's you."

IMOGEN

I somehow maintain my composure and keep my jaw from dropping. *This* guy? Flirting with *me*? This dark blond-haired, moss-eyed, full-bearded tall drink of water is hitting on bland, dark-haired, blue-eyed, curvy ol' me? No way.

I break our eye contact and laugh out loud to brush away my nerves. "Now, I'm not sure how your Australian girls react to that line, but *I'm* going to react by going back over there to my friends." I pick up the drinks that Cillian has finished and clear my throat. "Enjoy your time in Ireland, Mister...Um..."

"Robinson. And there aren't any Australian girls," he says with a wink. I stop myself from reacting. *How can a deep voice like that sound so...tender?* "No Irish girls either, by the looks of things."

I give a light-hearted chuckle to try and ease the increasingly awkward vibe. "I guess your game needs some work."

His eyes reconnect with mine, and my heart falls to my gut. "I suppose it does." He seems to be searching for something within mine, and I can't seem to break away. Suddenly, I hear a deep throat clear beside us, and I can't help but jump slightly.

It's Cillian. He places a tray filled with pints of dark stout next to the man, Mr. Robinson. "Your drinks, mate." His eyes flicker to mine, and I take it as my chance to leave the bar with my drinks. Bless Cillian's big, muscled—and probably tattooed—heart. He probably thought I needed help getting rid of the guy. But I'm not sure I did...or if I even *wanted* that interaction to end.

I arrive at the table with my friends who are giving me the *look*. Riley has her arms crossed and a big smirk on her lips. "So, who's the guy? Aren't ya gonna introduce us?" Molly and Saoirse burst into giggles.

I wave them off. "Ah, stop it, the lot of you. He's just some Aussie bloke looking for a quick, easy shag or something. You gals know I'm not that sort."

Molly's eyes follow movement behind me. "You can't deny that he's a fiiiine looking lad," she murmurs, earning a round of giggles from the rest of us.

The girls then start eyeing the pub for more eye candy to ogle and giggle about, so I take my seat and try my best not to search for the Australian stranger. Don't get me wrong, the fellow is absolutely *gorgeous*. However, anything with an obvious tourist can't be anything *but* the fuck-em, leave-em variety, and really, that's not my thing. I fall absolutely head over heels in love the instant my lips meet those of another, much less when having *sex*.

"So, who are we drinking to, gals?" Saoirse says, lifting her glass of classic Irish cider.

"What? Besides our beloved Saint Patrick?" I joke.

Riley scratches her chin, then her eyes light up as if remembering. "To our Imogen, of course! By the luck of Saint Paddy, may she nail tomorrow's job interview on the head!"

"Here, here!" we all say and clink glasses before taking sips of our respective drinks.

I nearly smack my head. *The job interview! Ugh...*

But, I struggle to leave the Getting Lucky pub. Riley's right, I haven't spent any time with the gals over the last couple of weeks because I've been so stressed about this interview tomorrow. Might as well give it a couple more hours.

The girls are debating about whether Magners or Bulmers is the better tasting cider—you know, important questions— when I start to feel an itch on my shoulder. I turn around and scan the room, only to find the Aussie guy looking at me. Butterflies flutter in my stomach and I can feel my face blush. Just who *is* this guy and how is he making me feel this way? I hear his friends giving him shit for drinking water instead of beer. I mean, yeah, that *is* a bit weird for someone to be in an *Irish* pub in *Ireland* on *Saint Patrick's Day* to *not* drink.

I turn my attention away from him before his friends catch me staring and bring it back to my girls. I've known the lot of them since nursery school, and we've all been inseparable ever since—Riley even more so, given that she's my roommate now. I feel a pang of guilt at what Riley said earlier back home. We would normally have our ladies' nights every Wednesday, and I've just not had the heart to come. Molly and Saorise, bless them, have been more understanding because they know I'm the fussy type. Riley, on the other hand, would never let me hear the end of things. But I still love her to bits.

Speaking of Riley...she's suddenly no longer at our table.

"Hey, where'd Riley go?" I ask Molly and Saoirse who simply point, mouths wide open.

I follow their eyes and spot Riley whooping and cheering in the middle of the pub, successfully rallying a bunch of people to dance the Irish jig with her. Aoife's turned the music up, and the pub's patrons start to form a circle around her and a couple of others, clapping to the beat.

"C'mon, lads and lassies! Here's to Paddy!" she hollers after taking another glug from her pint glass, red-faced, dragging more people into her jig-pit. She's always been a bit of a lightweight, but *jeez* I haven't seen her this rowdy since our graduation party.

Molly starts to get up and downs the rest of her drink before shouting, "All right, I'm sold. Let's go, gals!" She leaves the table and joins Riley.

Saoirse downs hers too and bursts into laughter. "Rally the lassies! Time to back our gal up!" She stands up but looks over to me before heading off. "Coming, Imogen?"

I hold my hands up in defeat. "I'll have to pass, lovely. I shouldn't be up much longer, I've got that interview tomorrow."

I start to stand up, and she pulls me into a big, bear hug before planting a big kiss on my cheek. "I getcha. Go knock 'em dead, lass. I'll catch you after then?"

"As soon as I'm done we'll have a riot of a night," I say, grinning and she leaves to join the rest.

I walk over to the big, old door that shields Getting Lucky from the outside world and place a hand on its thick wooden form. It's full of ridges and scratches from its years of life, but it's just as much a part of the pub as it is our little town of Duthmoore. When Cillian took over the property, he didn't have the heart to modernize anything about the place. I glance over my shoulder to the bar, spotting Cillian with a rare smile on his face although his arms are crossed. He may come off as the gruff sort, especially with his stature and tattoos, but really he's a big teddy bear, and we all love him the same.

I glance around the room one more time, taking in the love and positive energy of the place before pushing the door open and going back out into the cool March evening. Maybe I can still fit in an episode or two of Bridgerton before I call it a night.

LEO

I sit down at the table of our meeting room with a sigh, resisting the urge to slouch. I left Duthmoore for the day to sort out the interviews for Tru Blu's new Belfast team, and I'm already regretting it. My ears are still ringing from the festivities of the night before, but I'm relieved that I had the foresight not to drink at all. I'd most definitely be dragging my feet today if I did.

A knock sounds on the meeting room door. "Come in," I call out.

"Morning, Mr. Robinson, here's your morning order," the receptionist, Nora, greets me with a smile as she opens the door to the meeting room. She hands me a fresh cuppa, the smell of which wakes me up instantly. Still grinning, she walks back to the door, but before opening it she turns to me. "Shall I bring in the first candidate?"

I stretch out my fingers, causing some of my knuckles to pop before I move my head from side to side. Taking a deep inhale, then a slow exhale, I smile at her, feeling as ready as I'll ever be. "Sure. Let's get this started."

And I never regretted my words as much as I have those.

I pretend to read over the interviewee's resume in an attempt to not cringe at the preposterousness of his words. He's actually put on his resume that he was a dope dealer during high school, claiming it taught him entrepreneurial skills such as supply and demand, money management, and customer service skills. Seriously, who's *telling* these young kids that it's OK to say things like that on their resume, much less *in an interview*? I take a sip of my now luke-warm tea then look straight into the kid's eyes and cut him off from whatever he's saying. "That'll be all, thank you."

His face flushes in fear for a moment, but he quickly picks up a false sense of confidence and puffs up his chest. "So, I'm hired?"

I pinch my thigh to prevent myself from laughing before I gesture to the door, hoping that he understands there are still other candidates waiting outside. "We'll be in contact with any updates."

"Oh, sure." He jumps up from his seat. "I hope you have a great day."

I simply nod. "You too, mate." As he opens the door to the meeting room, I call out, "Next!" And my jaw drops when the curvy goddess from the pub last night enters looking like a dream come true. I cross my legs underneath the table to try and stop my dick from showing its appreciation.

Her eyes widen in surprise as she realizes who I am. "Oh, wow, um… Hello, sir," she stumbles on her words and blushes. "Hope you're not going to hold last night against me. I…" She presses her lips together and fidgets with the gold cross hanging about her neck. "It wasn't you. It's just that I'm not that kind of girl."

"And what kind of girl is that?"

"The kind who meets a guy at the pub and goes home with him that night."

"Is that what you thought I was trying to do?"

She bounces a shoulder. "An Australian in small-town Ireland isn't likely to be in it for the long haul."

"I see. Why don't you come in and shut the door behind you?" I gesture to the seats across from me. "I assure you that wasn't my intention last night. But I guess I came on a little too hard, and I'm sorry if I gave you that impression. Approaching women at bars isn't something I normally do. Which is why I'm obviously so bad at it..." I trail off then sigh. "I forget that I'm not as young as I used to be. You just...took me by surprise last night. I'm sorry if I offended you in any way. It won't happen again."

As she sits, she lifts her gaze from her lap and into my eyes, making my heart skip a beat. "I'm not offended," she says before smiling. "As long as last night doesn't stop me from getting the job?"

I shake my head as I breathe out a sigh of relief. "Honestly, I thought you'd run right back out when you realized who I was." I laugh, feeling the tension between us dissipate. "And to answer your question, no. The only thing that would stop you from getting the job is if you're as woefully unqualified as the last guy. He tried to convince me that selling pot made him an entrepreneur, and the one before him thought posting on his personal social media accounts since he was thirteen was enough experience to come in here and develop social media strategies for multinational companies."

"Oh, I would never think that," she says

as she pulls out her resume from her bag. "Besides, I've been posting since I was ten. So I've got three years on that guy." She hands me her resume with a serious face. My jaw falls open, and I'm not sure how to take her response until she starts laughing. "I have a BSc in Communication, Advertising and Marketing from the University of Ulster."

My eyebrows shoot up, and I take her resume, reading thoroughly. *Imogen Walsh. So, that's your name.*

I continue scanning the piece of paper. Not only has she got the right degree, she even graduated with honors. "Well, well, an honors graduate, to boot. Why didn't you just say so?" I ask, impressed.

"No reason. But the look on your face was absolutely worth it," she says with a grin.

I chuckle. "In that case, I have a feeling that your chances are quite high here." I hand back her resume before continuing, "How does starting this Monday work for you?"

Her jaw drops and her eyes widen. It takes her a moment to process my words, and when she realizes that I'm being serious, she jumps up from her chair. "Perfect!" She reaches across the table to shake my hand, her breasts fall forward slightly, and her cleavage becomes more prominent. I take a deep breath and mentally tell my dick to calm down before taking her hand.

"Great. Be back here Monday at nine sharp."

"OK. I'll see you on Monday then, Mr. Robinson," she says, shaking my hand enthusiastically before leaving the room and taking all the air out of it with her.

After she shuts the door, I drop my shoulders and sigh, looking down at the erection I quite obviously failed to prevent. *Thank god we didn't get glass tables. That would've been embarrassing.*

Imogen Walsh is as beautiful as she is smart, and my attraction to her is more than palpable. Hiring her is possibly a terrible decision, but she's qualified, and I'm not the kind to refuse a woman a position just because she doesn't want me in her bed. I'm man enough to accept that, and big enough and ugly enough to know when a woman is out of my league.

I glance over to where she was just sitting, wishing things were different but knowing it's better that they aren't. Office romances always turn messy anyway.

IMOGEN

"Have a nice day," I say to the receptionist, biting the inside of my cheek to help me keep my cool as I leave the Tru Blu offices.

The moment I get into the elevator though, I start bouncing up and down, my excitement threatening to burst out of me. Thankfully I'm alone, otherwise people might think I desperately need a wee. But I'm just so damn happy I need to bounce it out.

I spot my car in the parking lot and quicken my pace. As soon as I place my butt onto the driver's seat, I let out an excited squeal and pump my fists in the air. This is my first *proper* job since graduating from university. I'm stoked!

"Farewell, cruddy waitress jobs. Hello, adulthood! Ee-hee-heeee!" I holler and drum my hands on the steering wheel. "I'm gainfully employed, motherfuckers!"

Tap, tap, tap.

My heart drops to my stomach. And I turn my head to the source of the sound, only to find Mr. Robinson standing by the window. *Oh, Crap.* He gives me a small wave, and I roll down the window. I can see that he's trying his hardest not to laugh, though a smirk still plays at the corners of his mouth.

"Y-yes?" I squeak, my face on fire.

He hands me a large envelope and chuckles. "HR needs you to fill out this employee packet. You can give it back on Monday."

I clear my throat and narrow my eyes. "You saw *nothing* just now, understand?" I jab a finger on his stomach, hitting nothing but steel underneath his shirt.

He laughs and holds up his hands in surrender. "Mum's the word. Promise, I won't tell a soul."

I curtly nod. "Good. Thanks for the packet. I'll see you on Monday."

I roll up the window, stick the car into reverse, and get the heck outta Dodge, groaning out loud as I do. "*Whyyyy* do you always embarrass yourself like that, Imogen fricking Walsh? Jesus, Mary, and Joseph..." I kick myself mentally for not being able to maintain my composure, for not checking my surroundings before I had my little dance party in the car.

Leaving the garage, I sigh. I can't believe the Aussie hottie from the pub is my *boss*. It's going to be hell trying to concentrate on work with him being around. I'm going to have to see him *every single day* for the rest of my career now—or maybe not. He *is* Australian, and Tru Blu is a new company starting up in Belfast. He might leave to go back to Australia once it's all set up and running. He might never come back.

I have to stop thinking about him. I'm getting my knickers all in a twist when I know nothing could ever happen between us. He's my boss now, and he's likely to be jetting back to Australia at any moment. The only kind of relationship I can do is long term, head over heels, make me your wife, and let me have your babies kind of thing. So I need to get my head out of the clouds and quit fantasizing about him before it becomes a problem in the office.

"But he's *sooooo hot!*" I groan when I stop at the next traffic light and bury my head in my hands. *Don't do this to yourself, Imogen. You don't even know his first name. There will be other men to find your forever with...*

And that's the thing that gets me—*will*

there be another? Will there be another man who makes my whole body tingle the way that Mr. Robinson does? I've never felt this way before, not with any of my past relationships. This feeling is...surreal. Like fate. His mossy green eyes, marked by crow's feet, probably from years of laughter. His comically deep, accented voice that seems to just roll over my body, causing vibrations all over. And from what I felt under that shirt, he most definitely takes care of himself, despite his mature age...

Honk, honk!

The car behind me brings me back to the present, and I realize that the light turned green during my internal struggle. I stick my car into gear and head back to Duthmoore, mind still reeling from landing the job, body still pulsing from seeing Mr. Robinson in close quarters.

I wonder how much longer he'll be in Ireland for...

LEO

After attending a couple of meetings with contractors and finalizing everything for Tru Blu's official opening on Monday, I make my way back to Duthmoore to enjoy the rest of the weekend—a celebration of all the hard work it took to get here. A decade ago, Sam and I were a tiny marketing start-up running out of a spare bedroom in my house. Now, we're one of the world's biggest digital marketing agencies, opening up our first international office in Belfast. It's an exciting time worthy of celebration, so the boys have decided to head back to Getting Lucky for dinner. Conor and Sam both drank a little too much last night, so they're calling this 'returning to the scene of the crime for a little hair of the dog,' which just means they're planning on drinking at the same bar regardless of how hungover they are. We even sit in the same booth.

"So, Leo, how were the interviews?" Sam asks as Aoife brings over a massive stack of french fries as our appetizer. My stomach grumbles at the sight of the crunchy, straw-like stack. "Cheers, Aoife!" he says, earning a smile from the waitress.

When she is out of earshot, I let out a loud groan. "Don't get me started, mate. You're lucky that you weren't there. You probably would've exploded."

Finn snags a handful of fries. "What would've made whose head explode?"

"Our friend here apparently had a horrible day of interviews." Sam pats me on the back.

"Mate, there was a guy who thought that handling his own socials with less than *a thousand* followers each since he was thirteen was enough to qualify," I say, earning roaring laughter from the rest of the table. "And don't get me started on the 'entrepreneur'."

Conor takes a slug of his beer before asking, "Does that mean you need to do a second round of interviews?"

I sip my water and shake my head. "Nah, thankfully there was *one* good candidate. Hired her on the spot."

Cheers ripple across the table. Sam lifts his hand to bump mine and grins. "Good. I wouldn't have been able to handle going with you if there was another round of interviews." He lifts his glass. "Here's to Tru Blu Marketing!"

We all respond with a jolly, "Here, here!" before clinking our glasses together.

Aiden glances behind me and raises his eyebrows. "Hey, isn't that the girl you were eye-fucking last night?"

I turn around to see Imogen walking into the pub with a friend. My dick hardens. Our eyes lock, and her face immediately blushes up a storm. *Fuck, she's gorgeous.*

"I wasn't eye-fucking anybody," I say as I turn back to my friends and cross my arms.

Conor belches and laughs up a storm. "My arse, you weren't! You were looking at her all night!"

"Remember when he took a ten-minute 'bathroom break', and we saw him wandering the pub instead?" Sam chimes in, earning more laughter from the group.

"If you must know," I cut in. "I was just trying to soak up the atmosphere last night since you lot were rolling drunk. And there's nothing to talk about where that girl is concerned. Well, besides the fact that she's the girl I just hired."

Finn nearly chokes on the fries and turns to look at the rest of the boys, who look at each other quizzically. Finn sips on his beer and clears his throat. "Uhm... Leo, *a-mhac*," he starts, calling me the Irish equivalent of 'mate'—sounding *nothing* like it's apparently spelled, '*uh-wak*'. He clears his throat again. "Do we need to institute a no fraternization policy?"

I scrunch my face and scoff. "That won't be necessary, mate. I'm a big boy, I think I can control myself."

Conor snorts. "We'll see about that." He cups his hands together and yells. "Oi, lassies!"

My face starts to burn up, and I'm grateful to my beard for being able to hide it. "What the fuck are you doing, Conor?"

He glances at me and smirks. "I'm being nice to the new member of your team." He turns back to Imogen and her friend. "Come join us, will ya?"

I turn to the direction of Imogen and her friend who is looking at her questioningly. Imogen whispers something into her friend's ear and shrugs. Her friend looks at me, breaks into a big grin, and drags Imogen over. "Hello, lads, you called?" she says.

Sam chirps up. "I'm Sam. And this here's Conor, Finn, Aidan, and I'm sure you know

Leo." He points to each of us in turn. "We were wondering if you'd like to join us for a bit of a celebratory dinner—on us—seeing that your friend here has just landed a job at mine and Leo's company?"

Imogen opens her mouth to speak, but her friend promptly cuts her off. "Oh, how kind. We would love to!"

"Brilliant! Make some room, lads. C'mon, scootch over," Sam barks playfully, and the boys comply, moving over to make room for our two unexpected, but not unwelcome, table guests. Suddenly, I'm very, *very* jealous of Finn who now has Imogen plastered against his side. This girl sets off feelings inside me I've never experienced before. Having her work for the company is one thing, but spending time with her in a little Irish pub socially is another altogether. Silently, I curse Sam for calling them to our table. *This is a terrible, horrible idea.*

IMOGEN

"All right, this round's on me," Leo announces when our dinner plates are cleared. Finn and I shuffle out of the booth so he can head to the bar. "Cider again?" He checks with Riley and me, pointing at our empty glasses.

"Please," I say, about to sit back down when Riley kicks my foot. I almost yelp.

"Go help him," she mouths, subtly nudging her head in his direction. My nose flares and I shake my head, but she kicks me again.

"*Fine*," I mouth back and follow Leo to the bar.

Leo... No, better not call him that. He is your fricking boss now, Imogen...

He eyes me with question as I come over and lift my hands. "Just here to help with the drink carrying." I glance around the pub before continuing, "Aoife seems to be busy anyway."

He smirks and nods. "Thanks, I appreciate it." He flags Cillian down and clears his throat. "Three pints of Guinness please, mate, two ciders for the ladies, and a water for myself. Cheers." He finishes the order and Cillian simply nods.

Water again? I bite my lip but am unable to contain my curiosity. "You're only ordering water, Mr. Robinson?" I blurt before I can stop myself.

"Please, Imogen, no need to be formal—call me Leo."

My heart flutters. "You know my name?"

"Ahhh, I did read your resume, you know." He laughs good-heartedly, making my face blush.

"Oh, my god. I think that was the dumbest thing I've ever said. Ignore me. I'm just nervous. It's not every day that you go out to celebrate a new job only to run into the hot Aussie who hit on you the night before who also just happens to *be* your new boss. *Then* that new boss invites you to have dinner with his friends," I ramble before promptly clapping my hand over my mouth. "I'm sorry." I wince. "You make me nervous. I mean, I'm just nervous. You're fine. You're totally"—my eyes do a slow up and down over his tall, muscular form—"Fine." *Someone glue my lips together to keep me from speaking!* "I mean, you don't make me nervous. I'm just a nervous person when I'm around new people."

He looks at me for a beat then smiles. "OK. Good to know. I'll keep that in mind when introducing you around at the office on Monday."

"Oh great," I say, laughing way more than I'm supposed to in this situation. I sound a bit like a hyena and I really just wish I could stop, but then I snort, and suddenly I'm wishing the floor would just open up and swallow me. I clear my throat. "So, why are you ordering water at a pub, Leo?" You know, I like the way his name rolls of my tongue—short yet perfectly fitting for a man like him. He *does* look like a bit of a lion, in a way. With the beard and all. A tall, chiseled, *hunky* lion...*Rawr!*

"It's terribly anti-social of me, isn't it?" he says as he turns away and bites his lip. A heartbeat later, he looks deep into my eyes. "My family has a history of drinking problems— on both sides, believe it or not—so, I only drink in social situations and prefer not to drink more than one or two whenever I do. I don't like being drunk. " He breaks our eye contact, snapping me out of his unintentional spell. "I always get a lot of shit from my mates, even the ones who've known me for a while." He takes a deep breath and our eyes meet once more. "But it's my choice, so I stick with it. Fuck what other people think, right?"

"Right," I say, standing there with my mouth slightly agape. "Do you...do you think *you* have a problem?"

He frowns and shakes his head. "Wouldn't bloody know to be honest. But I'm not willing to push things and find out," he says, smirking. "If we don't grow from the mistakes of our parents, and their parents before, then we're truly fucked. That's the lesson life put in front of me, and I decided to take it to heart long ago."

"That's very brave," I say. "And responsible. And *mature*. Most people would just keep following the pattern. But I guess knowing your mind is what made your company such a big success."

He simply nods, and we stand there in silence, waiting for our drinks. I can't help but look at him in quiet admiration. What he just told me was extremely brave and the choice he made...I totally respect that. This man is a lot more than he looks. It takes a lot of courage and willpower - it isn't an easy thing to do. It's not easy for people to learn from the mistakes of others, and so many children tend to fall into the same addictive patterns as their parents. A curse? No. Just a vicious cycle that won't stop until one steps up like Leo has.

I wonder what else he's hiding behind that quietly confident exterior?

"So...Leo," my voice cuts through our comfortable silence.

"Here ya go," Cillian interrupts—again!—and hands us our drinks over on two trays.

"Cheers, mate," Leo says, picking up a tray. I promptly pick up the other, and with a nod, we make our way back to our table, gaining a round of applause for some reason.

Setting the trays down, both Leo and I slide into the end of the booth across from each other. Me next to Riley and him next to Finn. I can't keep my eyes from straying to him as he seamlessly rejoins the conversation. Riley leans in and tugs on my top to pull me in. "Hey, we're going to hang out at Conor's cottage. Apparently, his family's got one of them big bits of land."

I raise an eyebrow. "We? Don't I get a say in this?"

Riley rolls her eyes. "We're going. It'll be fun." I cross my arms before she rolls her eyes again and continues, "Conor says we can even go hunting with them this weekend. Isn't that a lark?"

My eyebrows furrow. "*You* want to hunt? *You*? Hunting?"

"Yeah, sure, why the heck not?" She gives me *the look*, flicking a glance between myself and Leo, then quickly at Finn. *Ohhhhhhhh...*

I simply bounce a shoulder. "Sure. Why not." I wiggle my eyebrows at her, causing her to smack my arm.

"All right, lads, let's get to it!" Riley woots before downing her cider, causing the rest of the table to hoot and holler before promptly chugging down their drinks.

I glance at Leo, who just smirks. The redhead, Conor, I think, belches after finishing his drink and smacks his pint glass onto our table. "You all right there, ya lightweight Aussie?" he says to Sam, who's only just taken a mouthful of his drink.

"Lightweight? Who you calling 'lightweight'? I'm simply enjoying my alcoholic beverage," he responds, taking another sip, his eyes moving to me in question as I slowly sip mine.

I lift my hands up. "I want no part in this."

Riley shoves me. "Hurry *up,* Imogen! We wanna go have some fu-un!" She sings the last word, and I have to wonder how much fun drinking and hunting with a bunch of blokes we don't know could be. Sounds like the plot of a horror movie to me. However, when I look over at Leo, I feel nothing but calm and a lot excited to spend more time around him.

"I could drop you home if you'd rather?" Leo says when our eyes lock across the table. "I'm obviously the designated driver here." He tilts his water to illustrate his point.

"Oh, no, I'm coming," I say, waving him off before I lean in close to him. "I need to keep an eye on my party friend Riley over there. Who knows what mischief she would be up to without me around." The smell of his cologne hits me like a wave, making my lady bits tingle happily. I have to hold back the need to shudder. And when he smiles, I have to refrain from wanting to take his face into my hands and kiss those thick lips. To feel the tickle of his full beard on my skin.

"In that case, you can sit up front with me."

LEO

As the chilliness of the March evening sets in, we set up a bonfire in Conor's yard, huddling around it and just shooting the shit, telling stories, and drinking to pass the time. Riley is sitting close by Conor, giggling and flirting, while Imogen is between Riley and me, looking a little awkward. I kind of wish she's huddle up next to me with the blanket she has draped around her shoulders the way Riley is huddling up to Conor. But I also know that's a terrible idea, so I just stay where I am, leaving a good meter in space between us.

"Riley? What are you doing?" Imogen asks her friend, who's texting suddenly frantically.

She peeps up from her phone with a

guilty look on her face. "Conor said it would be fine to invite some more friends over."

"Riley..." Imogen starts. "I thought you said this was just a 'hang out'?"

"It is," Riley says with a cheeky grin. "It's just going to be a bigger one now."

Imogen sighs and crosses her arms across her chest, making her breasts squeeze together. I have to look away because just a glimpse at the gorgeous cleavage of hers makes my pants feel tighter. It's not that I'm a sex-starved lunatic. It's just that Imogen is doing things to me I've never experienced before. We've barely even met, hardly know each other, but for some reason she's in my head, and possibly, in my heart. I want no one else, no, *nothing* else except her.

But I can't. We have a professional relationship now, and I can't allow my feelings to get in the way of Tru Blu's growth. The company needs her, and I need to put the needs of my company first. This insta-attraction I have toward her will go away if I just wait it out. Eventually...

"You don't like parties?" I ask, and Imogen shrugs.

"Not as much as Riley does."

Like magic, cars start to arrive as if they were waiting in the wings, and before I know it, this 'hang out' quickly turns into a full-blown party. There are now tens of people who've brought even more drinks with them. Music is playing from one of the cars, and people are dancing and grinding along to its beat.

Imogen holds a handful of conversations before she moves to the edge of the party, then walks away. I run a few steps to catch up with her. "Hey. Where are you off to?" I ask when I catch up.

"Away from all this," she says and then waves her hand across the increasing number of bodies. "Wanna walk with me?"

I glance back at the party and sigh. "I think I'd enjoy that," I say, zipping my jacket around me.

"Not a fan of parties either?"

I give her a smile and shake my head. "Not in the slightest."

"And yet your mates are all rather rowdy."

"The cost of doing business. Not all deals are done in the boardroom. Most business relationships are solidified over dinner, drinks, and sometimes, drunken party weekends in Duthmoore. I just hope the hunting part will either be forgotten or at least postponed until they all sober up."

"Maybe we shouldn't walk too far then," she says, giving me a smile that has my insides tightening. "Keep an eye on them so no one gets hurt."

"The responsibility of the sober ones."

She lets out a laugh as we settle in a quiet corner of the yard where there's a bench seat and the bonfire is still in view. "So..." Imogen starts, giving me a nervous glance.

"So..." I continue.

She sighs and bites her lips to hide her smile. "I'm really not that great at this small-talk game, either, if I'm honest with ya."

I chuckle. "More in common already. I like it. We don't have to talk at all if that works."

"I like talking. I just don't like talking about nothing. Like the weather for instance. Everyone's always talking about the weather like there's nothing else going on in the world."

I look up at the spotless sky and sigh. "Then I guess I shouldn't mention that I thought I'd be spending my time in Ireland getting rained on."

She laughs. "Oh, come on! Not you too. We're not *England*, ya know! We've got distinct seasons. We've even got sunny winters. Seriously, if I ever meet whoever came up with that one, they'll be getting a serious talking to. Did you know that Irish people actually go *swimming* in the summer? And it doesn't snow all winter either. Especially not up here in the north."

Listening to her ramble in her cute Irish accent makes me smile and my heart swell. That is a voice destined to make me happy for the rest of my life. And it's in this moment that I decide that I don't care if she works for me or not. Hell, if things get awkward in the office, *I'll* be the one to leave. All I know for sure is that if this gorgeous woman gives me a single hint that she's interested in me the way I'm interested in her, I'm going for it.

"You think the preconceptions about Ireland are bad? Try living where the world thinks everything is trying to kill you. If I have to explain that I didn't grow up constantly fending off the attacks of snakes and giant spiders one more time, I might jump on the bandwagon and start telling everyone I went surfing on the back of a saltwater crocodile."

She giggles. "Wait. You're telling me that doesn't happen?"

"Definitely not," I say with a chuckle.

"And you never went to the toilet to find a snake curled up inside it?"

"Never."

"What about spiders in your shoes?"

"Nope. I'm from Melbourne. Those snake and spider stories you see on the internet happen way out in the country areas or up in Queensland or the Northern Territory. It's like living in the tropics up there, so think Florida and their snakes and gators, and you'll have a comparison. The cities are much like anywhere else in the world—relatively wildlife-free."

She looks at me for a long moment. "Heh. I've been misled."

"You have." I lean in a little and nudge her with my shoulder. "We all have it seems."

She scratches her cute little chin in concentration. "What about kangaroos and koalas? Do you see them around?"

"You might come across a couple once you're out of the cities, or they might find their way to suburbia during bushfire season, but they're not *everywhere*...and no, no one keeps them as pets either—that's actually illegal."

Imogen pouts then sighs. "But koalas are so cute..."

"You can still see them in sanctuaries

and stuff. Pet them, feed them... Snap selfies," I add.

"Snap selfies? How old do you think I am—sixteen? I don't do selfies," she grumbles. "I'm way past that stage now, thank you very much."

"You're probably the only twenty-five-year-old on the planet not taking selfies these days. But thank God. I don't know how I could have lived if I'd unwittingly hired a selfie-addict," I say, making her expression morph into laughter.

"Read my resume rather thoroughly, huh?" She looks at me, curiously as if trying to figure out a puzzle on my face. "Well, fair's fair. How old are ya, anyway?"

I gasp in mock-shock. "Don't you know it's rude to ask a bearded man his age?" I say, and she bursts into laughter. I want to do this with her every day. My *soul* wants to. This tension, this...*need*, it's tearing me apart inside. *Just give me a sign, Imogen.*

"There are special rules for bearded men? I had no idea."

"Well, now you know." I flash her a smile then add, "I'm thirty-nine this year."

Her brows furrow. "You're lying."

"Nope. That's what it says on my license," I say, taking out my wallet, then my license, and handing it to her. "I'm pretty sure I'm not *that* terrible at math."

She takes my license out of my hand and scrutinizes it. "My word, you don't look a day over thirty. I would never have guessed," she says, visibly taken aback. She hands me my license, and I feel that hope of mine start to waver.

"Is me pushing forty a problem?"

She blushes as if I just caught her doing something she shouldn't, and turns away from me, fidgeting with the edge of the blanket she has around her still. "Oh, no. Not at all. Why would I be bothered about the age of my boss? You could be twenty or a hundred, and it wouldn't change anything. I work for you. And to be honest, I'm just happy even *having* a proper job."

"Yeah. Your boss." Her words sink in like a lead weight in the pit of my stomach. I've never been great with women. I'm awful at knowing how to read the subtle signs that tell me whether they're interested or not. I take shyness or nervousness on their part as meaning I should go away. Guys like Sam and Conor just look at a girl and know if they're 'in' or not, but me…I have no fucking clue. Probably why I'm almost thirty-nine and still single.

She finally turns back to face me, and

the mood between us feels tense and unsure. Her lips part slightly as she scans my features and I'm caught between fight and flight. "Tell me more about Australia."

"Sure you don't want to keep this focused on work since I'm your boss now?" I ask, her answer determining my next move.

"We can talk work at work. But here... it's a party, and I could honestly listen to your voice for hours." She lifts her eyes to mine then smiles. "I love how deep and warm it is."

"Seriously?" A burst of nervous laughter comes out from me as I turn away from her and scrape a hand down my beard. "I'm actually really self-conscious about it. It's comically deep. I got called 'Froggy' a lot back in my schooling days."

"Kids are mean." I feel her hand on my arm which makes me turn back toward her. "But I really do mean it when I say that I love your voice. It's...sexy."

My brow hits my hairline as I search her eyes. "What happened to me being your boss?"

"Well, you *did* tell me I was the reason you came to Ireland *before* you became my boss. And if I'm honest here, the only reason I walked away from you was because

I thought you were just a tourist. I don't, er....I don't take part in flings."

"Neither do I," I say, my heart pounding in my chest as hope turns into destiny.

"No?" There's a look in her eyes, one that gives me a shit ton of hope.

"No," I admit, my tongue wetting the seam of my lips as I glance at hers. "And since we're being honest here, I...I don't just want to be your boss, Imogen. I'd like to be a lot more than that."

Her breathing deepens as her eyes linger over my lips then flicker back to mine, a hunger inside them that matches my own. "I really want to kiss you now," she whispers as she leans closer into me. There's a tiny moment of hesitation before our lips graze against each other's, the risk we're taking thickening the air and creating this invisible wall. And then, just as suddenly as it appears, we break it down, crashing our lips together as her hands grab at my jacket and my arms wrap around her body.

My hand slides up her back and into her hair, tugging her back as my tongue demands entry. Her lips feel like velvet, and her tongue tastes like honey. Never has a meeting of mouths felt so right, as if our lips were made for each other from the get-go, as if the only reason I lived my life so far was to make it to this moment. "Imogen," I rasp against her mouth, my entire body wanting more than just this kiss.

BANG!

We jump apart. "What the hell was that?" Imogen gasps.

I set my jaw. "Fucking idiots," I growl, instantly getting to my feet.

IMOGEN

"Was that a gun?" I yell after another explosion goes off in the distance.

Leo pulls me into his arms protectively and scans the area. "They are actually insane. Is that...*laughter*?"

I don't respond and instead cock my head to the side to listen in to the silence following the sudden boom. There *is* laughter in the distance...and cheering. What the hell is going on?

"I hear it too," I finally say. "Should we go and investi—" *BANG!* I let out a scream and cover my ears.

"We'll need to go talk some bloody sense into them before someone gets hurt." Leo presses his mouth together in a straight line, and I have to admit I'm crazy turned on by this take-charge side of him, which only serves as a reminder that we just made out not sixty seconds ago. Ohmi*gosh*. I just fucking kissed my boss! I haven't even started my first real job and I'm already jeopardizing it. What on earth is wrong with me?

BANG! The next shot is followed by a massive cheer on top of the laughter.

"Come on," Leo says, taking my hand in his and heading toward the sound. I'm of two minds about this. Firstly, I'm not a big fan of guns and would prefer to run away from, not *to* them. But secondly, I do really like having this big, brawny Aussie tugging me along protectively. Everything about Leo makes me feel safe and secure, so crazily, I'm OK with going *toward* the chaos as long as it's with him.

After following a few more gunshots, Leo and I arrive in a big open field and spot the group gathered around a central figure—obviously the person with the rifle. And as we get closer and closer to the group, I come to realize the person holding the rifle is none other than my best friend. "What the actual hell?" I stop in my tracks, and Leo releases my hand. To my knowledge, Riley has never even held a fecking rifle, let alone shot one! This is a disaster.

"PULL!" Riley yells as she takes aim into

the dark sky. A clay pigeon comes flying from the side and above the gathered group. *BANG!* Riley fires, her slight body jolting back at the recoil as the bullet launches into the sky and...totally misses. "That's bullshit! I definitely hit that one." She pouts before walking into the arms of Conor, who hugs her and kisses her on the forehead. *No big shock there.*

Leo sighs. "This is reckless. We need to call it off before the cops come."

"Agreed. Just...be careful...boss."

His brow lifts and his eyes cloud over. "I'm your boss again?"

"I—"

"PULL!" *BANG!*

"Shit," Leo hisses, shaking his head before he moves toward the group with me following close behind, our conversation obviously postponed for now. "All right, guys. I know we're all having a great time, but I think we need to call it a night—at least with the shooting. None of us needs the cops showing up here."

"Oh, boo! Party pooper!" Riley moans from the arms of Conor, and some of the group murmur in agreement.

"Shooting things isn't a party, Riley." I cross my arms and shake my head, backing Leo up. "I don't care what the fuck you think. I'm not interested in spending the night in a cell just because you fecking eejits thought it'd be fun to shoot weapons in the dead of night. Are you all mad?" I look from face to face, earning a bigger murmur of agreement from the group.

"OK," Finn agrees, seemingly the most sober of them all. "We'll pack all this away until tomorrow. Sound fair?"

Leo nods. "I think that would be wise."

"Ah, Leo, the big hairy lion," Conor slurs. "Always the responsible one saving us all from ourselves. Party's done, folks. On ya way." He flicks a hand in the air, and there's a slight grumble and muttering of goodbye as everyone clears out and heads home or to the next party. I don't care which.

"We should probably go too, Riley," I say, turning to my inebriated friend, who replies by turning to Conor.

"C'mon, handsome. Let's take our party elsewhere," she says in a sultry tone.

Conor grins and scoops her in his arms. She squeals, and I'm left standing there, watching them walk to the cottage as I sigh. "Looks like she's spending the night," I say, mostly to myself.

"I could drive you home if you'd like?" Leo offers, appearing by my side. "She'll be

OK here. Conor's not going to do anything she's not willing to do."

"Oh, Riley would never do anything she's not into. But Riley is also into many things. So..." I press my lips together and shake my head. "We're very different people."

"I can see that." He offers me a smile and warmth pools in my belly. "Let me get my keys and I'll get you home."

I shake my head and turn to face him for the first time since we kissed earlier. "No. I...I think I want to stay. If that's all right with *you*, of course. Now that the danger is over, I kind of don't want this night to end."

His mouth opens slightly in surprise, but he shuts it just as quickly and smiles instead. "Anything you want," he says in that glorious brogue of his.

I grin and rake my teeth over my bottom lip. "In that case, maybe we can go back to that fire and talk some more. I'm still waiting to hear more about where you grew up."

"OK," he says, offering me the crook of his elbow as the last of the cars leave the property, and Leo and I are suddenly all alone.

LEO

I grab a couple of blankets and place one on the ground near our only source of heat before I grab a few more logs and add them to the pit to feed the dwindling fire.

"Hey, is there a stick or something by you?" I ask over my shoulder.

Imogen searches around her vicinity and finds the long stick Conor used earlier, handing it to me so I can stoke the fire back to life. I stand up and dust off my hands. "There we go."

Setting the stick aside, I take a seat on the blanket next to Imogen. She smiles then looks up into the clear night's sky. I follow suit, then whistle in admiration. "I love nights like these," she murmurs. "It reminds me a lot of my childhood."

"How so?" I ask, gazing at her profile.

There's a twinkle in her eyes and a faint smile on her plump lips. *God, I want to kiss her again.*

She slowly closes her eyes, and her smile grows. "My *móraí* used to take my brother and me out camping when I was a wee lass. We'd lie out under the stars and tell stories about mystical creatures while eating marshmallows," she says, pausing for a moment as she turns to look at me.

"Who's your...mo-ray?" I ask.

She giggles. "Not 'mo-*ray*', 'mo-*ree*'. That means 'grandpa' in Gaelic."

"Ahhh...that makes sense," I start, then shake my head at myself and laugh.

She smiles at me sweetly. "Both my father and grandpa insisted that we learned Gaelic growing up. They were quite adamant that we keep the culture alive, and I'm glad that they did that."

I cock my head to one side. "Do all the Irish speak Gaelic?"

Her mouth turns into a disappointed frown, and she shakes her head. "No, not as many as there used to be." Imogen sighs and slumps her shoulders. "It's hard enough for *me* to find someone to practice speaking it to. I mean, my brother and I still use it as our secret language—even when texting—but that's not enough. I really hope I don't lose my touch. It's definitely something I want to pass on to my children one day."

At the mention of children, our eyes lock and hold oh-so briefly, but she quickly flicks hers away and looks back to the sky. *I would happily father her children. They'd be as beautiful as she is.*

"Did you go camping often?" I ask, noticing a slight movement in her body as she sucks a shivery breath between her teeth.

"Whenever we could." She pulls the blanket around her. "Gosh, it's cold."

"You're shivering, you poor thing. Want to head inside?"

"No," she says immediately.

"Then come here," I say as I pull her closer, wrapping my arms around her. Her body quivers against mine, then as our warmth intermingles, she relaxes into me with a sigh.

"Tell me about your childhood," she asks sleepily. "Everyone talks about Australia like it's a surfing paradise. What was it like to grow up there—the teasing aside, of course."

I release a heavy sigh as I draw her in closer. "My childhood was far from idyllic, unfortunately. You really don't want to hear about it, it's depressing."

"But I do. I want to know everything about you. If you don't mind talking about it of course."

Swallowing hard, I let my focus go soft as I guard myself against memories I don't need surfacing, preferring to stick to cold, hard facts. "Both my parents were alcoholics. So, I had to fend for myself most of the time. I think I cooked my first Kraft mac and cheese when I was five."

"Oh, gosh. I'm so sorry. What an awful thing to go through."

I bounce my shoulder slightly. "I don't even blame them. Alcoholism is a tough demon to fight. I'm just glad that they didn't decide to have more children."

"It's no wonder you're as brave and reliable as you seem. Having to take care of yourself all your life would have made you far more mature than you needed to be."

"Must be why I seem like such an old man then," I tease.

"No. You don't seem old at all. The impression I get from you is that you're solid, dependable—that you're a man who knows what he wants and works his arse off to get it."

I can't help but chuckle. "I'm not sure if that's a compliment or not, but you've definitely got my number."

She lifts her head. "That's how you'd describe yourself too?"

"Dependable? Yes. I'm not a man who takes many risks. But I am a man who knows what he wants."

"And what do you want?"

I reach up and tuck her long, dark hair behind her ear before wrapping my hand around the back of her head. "I want you," I whisper, bringing her mouth to mine.

IMOGEN

His mouth moves against mine with hungry passion. Never have I been kissed so surely and thoroughly. He takes control of my senses and makes me feel so wanted and adored that my emotions swell and I cling to him like I'm never letting go. We roll together so my back is against the ground and he's holding himself over me. There is a hunger in his eyes, his breath as heavy as mine. Electricity buzzes beneath my skin, and my body promptly shivers in excitement for more. My core aches, wanting more from this moment—wanting *everything* from it—as I let my legs fall open then rise up to meet the impressive bulge in his pants that tells me he wants this as much as I do.

"D-do you have a room?" I whisper in between kisses.

He hesitates before lifting his head to look at me. "Are you sure you want to—"

"Yes," I cut him off. "I know what I want too." I smile as I stare deeply into his eyes.

"Guess that makes two of us then." He chuckles as he effortlessly lifts me off the ground and kisses me before slowly lowering me to my feet. "This way."

Once inside the cottage, he takes us through a series of winding halls, our lips meeting and parting as we make our way to his room, a simple guest quarters with a double bed, a chest of drawers, and a single chair as furniture.

The door closes and we're on each other again, kissing and touching as we make our way toward the bed. Fireworks explode all over my body, and I'm about ten seconds away from ripping my clothes off for him to do with me as he pleases, but there's a voice in the back of my head that needs a little attention before we take this any further. "Wait," I say as I pull away and look into his eyes. "Is this going to affect my job at all? Because I really need that job..."

He laughs, causing my insides to melt through the deep bass of his voice. "No, not at all," he replies, grinning. "I'll even see to it that I'm not your direct supervisor."

"Good," I say, as a hungry smile spreads

across my face. "Because I really want to do this."

"Me too," he says as I grab the front of his shirt and we both fall on the bed. Our lips crash, the heat between us turns up to eleven, and we have no plans on slowing down.

His tongue pushes its way into my mouth, and it slides and prods against mine. The ache I feel for him, the *need* for him, grows larger and larger with every second that passes. Our tongues dance together in passion, round and round. My hands wander through his thick hair, then down his muscular body, while his roam down my curves and grip at my arse.

He pulls us apart, and there's a deep hunger in his eyes. "Take your clothes off," he demands in a low growl.

I nibble on his lip and smirk. "Why don't you do it for me?"

"My fucking pleasure," he murmurs into the crook of my neck, breath hot and heavy. He lifts my sweater, and I sit forward to help him take it off. His hands wrap around my back, and he expertly unclasps my bra, causing it to fall off onto the bed.

He leans back and sucks in a heated breath at the sight of me. "Fuck, you are absolutely breathtaking," he says, making my face flush.

"N-no I'm not. Don't be ridiculous," I stammer.

"I'm not being ridiculous," he murmurs, leaning back toward me, taking my lips into his once more. "You are the most beautiful thing I have ever seen, Imogen." He pauses and takes his own shirt off. But before I can marvel at the perfection that is *his* body, he immediately starts kissing me deeply once more.

I moan into the kiss, grinding up against him. His cock is rock hard underneath his jeans, and from what I can feel, *huge*, making the temple between my legs pulse with pure desire. "Leo, please," I whisper as I pull us apart again.

"Tell me, what do you want, my precious flower?"

Instead of answering, I reach between us and slowly start to unbutton his jeans, all while staring into his deep green eyes. *I could get lost in those forest gems forever.* He sits back, and I tug down his jeans along with his boxers, and he steps out of both. A long thick shaft jumps out from the confines of his pants, the sight of which makes my eyes widen in surprise.

"What's wrong?"

Shaking slightly with nerves, I wrap my hand around his rock-hard girth, my fingers not even meeting on the other side. "T-this. It's pretty...b-big."

"Are you worried I'll hurt you?" He hisses through his teeth as I pump my hand up and down his shaft. I love the way his big, manly chest heaves, and a bead of arousal forms on his tip. I rub the pad of my thumb over it.

"A little. But I don't want to stop what we're doing."

"OK," he whispers, pulling me to my feet again so I'm standing in front of him now, my breasts brushing against his chest. "I'll make sure you're good and ready for me." He lowers his hands to the waist of my jeans as he kisses me, long and slow as he unbuttons the fly and pushes the denim and my cotton panties past my hips. "I would never ever dream of hurting you, Imogen. You have my word that we'll go slow."

"I'd like that," I whisper, stepping out of the last of my clothes. I have a sudden moment where the reality of standing naked in front of my boss hits me, and nervous energy skitters about inside my belly. But those nerves are quickly replaced with heated arousal as he lowers me back to the bed, kissing me while his hand wanders down my body to the space between my legs. "Oh! Ohmigod." I melt into his touch as his thick fingers slide into my seam.

"You like that?" He glides his finger up and circles my clit.

"I do," I gasp.

"Mmm, I love how wet you are. You want more?"

"Yes."

He shifts down my body, kissing and licking my skin until he's settled between my legs, pushing my thighs wide before he buries his face into my valley. His tongue darts out and swirls around my clit, sucking and teasing. I arch my back and slide my fingers into his hair, burying his face deeper as I rock against him. "Ah! More, please, more. Don't stop, " I beg.

Releasing an erotic hum, he growls before he doubles down, sucking back harder as his fingers circle around my entrance before sliding in. One feels like two, and two feels like four, so when he adds a third, my walls are stretching and I'm gasping, both at the pleasure and the intrusion.

"*Fuuuuuuck*. Yes. Please, don't stop. Keep —ah! I think... I think I'm gonna..." I try to finish my sentence, but I can't. My back automatically arches further, and my fingers tighten against the back of his head, pushing his face even deeper into me. "Leo!" I moan as I hit my climax, my head thrashing about on the pillow as he draws every last wave of pleasure out of me. "Oh, God!"

As he brings me back down, he nuzzles his face into my dripping wet seam, slurping up my juices like a thirsty lion at a pond. "Fuck me, you taste so good," he murmurs into my crevice.

He reluctantly pulls himself away from me, and I can see that his cock is throbbing even harder than before. Could it possibly have just *enlarged?* I gulp. *No, I must be imagining things.*

"I want to drown my cock in your body," he growls. "And *I* want to feel you pulse around me as I fuck you senseless."

"Oh yes," I gasp.

"You ready for me?" He climbs back on top of me and hovers himself over my entrance.

"More than ready. Fill me, Leo," I murmur as our hungry eyes meet once more.

"Fuck, you amaze me," he says, and he slowly, finally, pushes himself into me.

I gasp, tears hitting my eyes as I stretch around his thickness. "*Ohhhhh...*" is all I manage to say before he pushes himself *all the way*. The sting burn gives way to a blissful feeling of completion. Like I never knew what being filled was until this moment. "You fit. My gawd. It feels so good."

He nibbles the crook of my neck again and whispers into my ear, "I think we were made for each other, Imogen." He slowly pulls himself out, and back in again, moaning in the process. "And I'm going to enjoy every fucking second of this."

He starts with slow thrusts, and with each moan that escapes my mouth, his movement becomes faster and faster. Our bodies move in sync, my hips meeting him thrust for thrust. I struggle to keep my shit together, and I climax again after a couple more thrusts. "Ah, *fuckkkkk*!" I moan. "Leo!"

"Oh, God, Imogen..." he says in between gasps. "I can feel you pulsing around my cock. *Fuck*. I don't know how much longer I can handle you."

"Don't stop. Don't *fucking*—ah!—stop, Leo." Wave after wave of pleasure erupts throughout my body as he thrusts and thrusts, keeping my climax going until it tumbles into yet another. "Ohhhhhh!"

"Imogen, *fuck*. I'm going to explode," he gasps as he pivots his hips, faster and faster than I ever thought possible.

My eyes roll back after yet another orgasm erupts throughout my body. "Fuck! *Leoooo*..."

"Imogen!" He collapses next to me on the bed, panting hard. "Holy fuck ...that was..."

"...absolutely incredible," I finish.

"Yeah," he gasps, laughing like he can't believe what just happened. And honestly, I can't either. This is the kind of sex you only hear about and never experience, or even think you'll ever experience—unless of course, you're lucky enough to meet your soulmate... *Could it be?*

Leo wraps his arms around me and kisses me long and slow. It feels so *right*, being like this with him. He makes me feel safe and secure and...loved. Which is what I think is happening here.

"Leo?" I whisper, pulling back slightly so I can look into his face.

"Imogen?" he responds with a smile. He reaches up and brushes his long fingers through my dark hair before settling his open palm against my naked back.

"Do you believe in..." I press my lips together, not sure I want to wear my hope and vulnerability out in the open.

"In what? God? Ghosts? Leprechauns? Fairies?" He smiles as he looks into my eyes, waiting for me to go on.

"Soulmates," I say finally. "Do you believe they exist?"

He takes a deep inhale as his eyes move between mine before he nods slightly. "Yes," he whispers. "I do."

My heart swells in my chest as he draws me in and presses a kiss against my forehead, wrapping me up tight like he never wants to let me go. And I don't want him to. As his breathing slows and I snuggle into the crook of his neck, I decided I could quite happily stay right here in his arms forever.

And it's only then that a final complication hits me. How long is he planning on staying in Ireland?

LEO

BANG!
 I shoot up to a seating position. "What the fuck?" I groan, rubbing the whiplash away from my neck. As my brain slowly gets out of the fog of sleep, I realize that my bed is empty. I turn my head, left and right - there's not a sign that she was ever here.

Except the scent of her on my sheets.

I *know* she was here and I *know* we had sex this morning. *But why did she leave without a word?*

I take a look at the digital clock on my bedside table - *1:30 pm*. "Ah, shit," I groan into the empty room. I slept most of Sunday away. I need to head back to Belfast before long.

BANG!

I slowly get out of bed and put on some

clothes. Maybe she's outside with the rest of them? At least, I hope she is. *God, I really hope she is.* I only just found her, and there's no way I'm even close to being done with her. Not yet, and probably not ever. I know without a doubt that there's something very special about this girl. *I was drawn to Ireland to find her...*

BANG!

I open the back door to find it's just the boys shooting clay pigeons in the yard—no girls in sight. My heart falls to the pit of my stomach. The amount of disappointment that seeps into and spreads throughout my body is unexplainable. I can't believe after all that, she would just up and leave without a word.

As if it could make her disappear from my thoughts, I shake my head then take a deep breath before I straighten up my shoulders and head toward the boys.

BANG!

I stop myself from cringing at the gunshot, much louder now than before as I make my way closer to the source. "Oi! What's going on out here?"

"Top of the morning to ya!" Conor says, tipping his pretend hat.

"Hey! Sleeping Beauty finally awakens," Finn says.

I shrug nonchalantly. "Long night," I say. "And we're down two ladies, I see. What's up with that?"

Sam shares a look with Finn and Aidan. Then the three of them look at Conor, who looks at the ground. "Uh, yeah. They left a bit ago," Sam answers. "Conor and Riley didn't get along as well in the cold light of day."

I glance at Conor. "What'd you say to her?"

"Nothin'," he responds, lifting a cigarette to his lips. "I'm just not about to marry the girl because we got drunk and fucked."

"You are *actually* the reason dating is so hard these days," Aiden says as he loads the thrower with more clay targets.

"Speaking of. It's not like you to fall into bed on the first date," Sam says, handing the rifle to Finn as he steps closer to me.

I shrug. "There's just something about this one."

He claps his hand on my shoulder. "Well, as long as it doesn't cause trouble at the office, I'm all for it. Wanna shoot with us?"

"Nah. Thought I might just go for a walk. Get a coffee or something."

"She said to tell you, see you Monday," he says as I walk off. And I nod, thanking him but feeling like maybe I read into what was between us more than I ought to.

~

"Good morning, Mr. Robinson." Nora greets me as I walk through the glass doors of Tru Blu on Monday morning.

"G'day, Nora. Good weekend?"

She beams. "Lovely, actually. And yourself?"

Stuffing my hands into my pockets, I chuckle. "I'm still deciding," I reply, gaining a look of confusion before she laughs politely. The phone starts to ring, saving her from my cryptic comment. "Tru Blu Marketing, how may I help you?"

Giving her a polite nod, I head into the main office and find myself automatically walking toward Imogen's new office. I already know that I shouldn't be bringing personal matters into the office but since I've had no way of contacting her since yesterday—her resume with her phone number and address remained at the office—I feel like this is my only opportunity to make sure we're both on the same page where our relationship is concerned.

I also have to admit that my ego is somewhat bruised since she left without saying goodbye. I felt *so* certain that she liked me as much as I like her. But since my radar on these things is sucky at best, I have to wonder if I was seeing things that weren't there.

Slowing as I come to her open door, I lift my hand and knock on the door frame, clearing my throat. She jumps three feet off her chair in surprise. "Oh, hi..." she squeaks when she turns her head toward me, and her face erupts in flames.

"Hey, Imogen. I was hoping we could talk," I say as I step into her office and shut the door behind me. "Privately."

"Oh. Uhm, y-yeah sure. Take a seat." She gestures to the spot close to her.

I stand in front of her desk and fold my arms protectively across my chest. "About this weekend..."

Her shoulders tense up. "Oh, God. I was really hoping we didn't have to do this talk." She sighs. "I woke up feeling totally embarrassed. I don't normally throw myself at men like that. I normally date first—a few dates, ya know? And flings with men who come from overseas are *never* part of my repertoire. And I would never normally go to bed with my boss, but you are super hot, and I'm obviously very weak around you. I promise

I won't make any of this awkward for you."

I furrow my brows and move my hands onto my hips. "Who said that was a fling?"

"Wasn't it, though?" she asks and then shakes her head. "How could it be anything but when you'll one day have to leave for Australia?"

"Who said I'm going back to Australia?" I ask in return.

"Well…no one. But…you *are* Australian, right? Sam said he'll be on the first flight back to Melbourne as soon the Dublin office is up and running. So that's, what? A week? Maybe two?"

"I'm not going back," I say, sliding my hands to my waist as I let out a relieved breath. Seems obvious that while I slept like the dead dreaming of a future with Imogen, she was out talking to my mates and getting a bunch of information that isn't even relevant to our situation. She left because she thought we could only be temporary.

Her jaw drops. "Y-you're not?"

"I'm not. Sam is, but not me. I'm staying in Dublin," I say, making her break into a smile, tears even forming in her eyes.

"Oh, gosh. You have no idea how happy I am to hear that."

"Look, Imogen, I like you. Like really,

really like you. I thought I made it clear that I don't do flings either."

"You did." She sniffs. "I just...I thought maybe I misunderstood that part when Sam was talking about going home. I thought you were going too. And I needed to protect my heart, because..." She sighs. "This sounds so over the top and crazy, but I could feel myself falling for you, and I didn't want to spend any more time with you if you were just gonna leave me. So I left instead."

"It's OK," I say, taking her hand in mine before continuing. "But since I'm staying, I'd really like to date you."

She squeals and then jumps up from her chair, wrapping her arms around my neck. "It is *more* than OK with me," she says before kissing me deeply, her entire body melting against mine. "I'd love nothing more than to date you, Leo Robinson."

"I have a feeling this is going to become more than just dating, Imogen. Especially if you believe in soulmates."

"Oh, I do. I do," she says, smiling, laughing, and crying all at the same time. I kiss her again and again, her giggles turning into moans as my body reacts in kind.

"Maybe we should keep the PDA for outside working hours though," I say, clearing my throat as I slowly release the grip I currently have on her arse.

"Orrrr, you could lock that door and fuck me on my desk," she purrs, causing me to seriously consider it.

"Don't tempt me, lass," I say in my best Irish accent, causing her to burst into another fit of giggles.

"Oh, I want to tempt you, Leo. I want to tempt you again, and again, and again."

Grinning, I pull her into my arms and hug her tight, my heart exploding in happiness and complete bliss. When I first made the decision to move all the way across the world, I did it thinking that it was all about growing my business. But the moment I laid eyes on Imogen, I knew. The reason I moved my life here was for her—my beautiful, buxom Irish lass. Call me old-fashioned, but I think I've finally found the one. She is right here, in my arms.

And I'll be damned if I don't work my arse off to keep her.

EPILOGUE 1

IMOGEN

Five years later...

"Mammy, Mammy, look! A rainbow!" Ollie, our little four-and-a-half-year-old, screams excitedly from Leo's shoulders.

"Whoa, there, Ollie. Do you think there's a pot o' gold at the end of it?" Leo asks, in his fake Irish accent, earning an amused look from me. His accent is the *worst*. But then, I'm terrible at mimicking his Australian accent too.

Ollie squeals again. "Can we check, can we check, can we check?"

"I don't know..." I start.

Ollie pouts. "Mammy, pleeeeaaaaasssseeeeee, can we go see if there's a pot o' gold?" He flashes his big blue eyes at me, my eyes. He most certainly knows how to tug at my heartstrings—a trait I'm sure he's picked up from his father.

I sigh and stand on my tiptoes to pinch his cheeks. "Well, all right then. You go off with Daddy." I blow a kiss at Leo, who gives me a wink in return.

"Daddy, Daddy, let's go, let's go, let's *go*!"

"All right, settle down up there, mate. You're gonna give Daddy's shoulders some big ouchies," Leo says as he puts Ollie onto his feet. Before we even know it, Ollie speeds off into the direction of the rainbow, further into the Irish greens.

"Oliver Robinson, don't run off like that without your Da!" I yell, then sigh and shake my head, knowing that my words would fly right over Ollie's head. He is so much like I was when I was a kid—so carefree and full of energy. I'm surprised my parents managed, but I'm absolutely loving it. Leo stands behind me and massages my shoulders, causing the tension to melt away.

"He can't go far. He'll run right back here in about thirty seconds." We watch, and lo and behold, Ollie stops running, slaps his little hands against his thighs like he's done with this chasing rainbows business before he turns back to us. "See? That little hellion runs out of puff pretty fast."

I turn around to meet his eyes, smiling

at me with complete and utter admiration. I stand on my tiptoes to kiss him deeply, enjoying the rush of electricity that shoots through my being every time I kiss him. We've had a whirlwind of a relationship since the moment he asked me to be his girlfriend smack at the beginning of office hours at Tru Blu. About two months into our new relationship, I realized that I had missed a few periods. We immediately took a pregnancy test and found out I was pregnant with who would turn out to be the most beautiful, bouncing baby boy. Leo proposed to me the very next day.

At first I thought he only proposed *because* I was pregnant. But turns out that he was really waiting for the right moment to pop the question because he had bought the ring about a week into our relationship. He was walking along the street in Belfast one day and saw the ring in a window display. He said he felt his heart sing at the look of it and had immediately imagined how it would look on my hand—so he bought it then and there.

We scrambled to get all the wedding arrangements sorted, and luck of the Irish on our side, we managed to organize an absolutely *gorgeous* wedding in Hawaii about two months after he proposed. Hawaii was the perfect middle-point for Leo's and my family to fly over, and they all made it. I had Riley as my maid-of-honor, of course, and Sam was Leo's best man—much to Riley's dismay as she wanted to walk down *our* aisle with her man Conor because it turns out that he *did* want more than just one night with her. They've been as inseparable as Leo and I since.

"Ewwwww, Mammy, Daddy. Get a room!" Ollie yells, making Leo and I break apart with a laugh.

"Ollie!" Leo gasps. "Where did you even hear that from?"

He giggles. "Auntie Saoirse says it all the time to Auntie Riley and Uncle Conor when they kiss. I think it's funny."

Leo leans over and whispers into my ear, "Well, I can see why *they* get told off." I giggle in response. "All right, Ollie," Leo starts. "Let's go see if we can find that pot o' gold together then."

"*Finally*," Ollie says, sounding a *bit* too much like his Auntie Riley there. He takes Leo's hand, comes to me and pulls me down, kisses me on the cheek and says, "*Tá grá agam duit*, Mammy." Which is, 'I love you' in Gaelic. "Daddy and I are going to look for gold for you now!" Then, he starts to march off into the distance with his father in hand who mouths 'Love you' as he gets tugged along.

I shake my head, smiling. My two men. The two loves of my life. Leo has been the perfect partner from the get-go, and he fit into the father role like a glove from the moment Ollie was born. As if he was just *meant* to be a dad. I told him that once while he expertly changed Ollie's diapers and he couldn't stop smiling for a week. Me, I can't stop smiling at all. Life with my men, it's perfect.

EPILOGUE 2
LEO

Ten years later...

"All right, Oliver, Seán, Thomas, let's get our shoes on or you're going to be late for your last day of school!" Imogen shouts from the front of our house, and the sound of three pairs of feet shuffling against the floor from the kitchen proceeds. I lean against the entrance to the kitchen to see my boys off.

"Are you coming for the Christmas concert, Ma?" Ollie asks. "Pack sunscreen if you are. It's outside."

"And a hat!" Thomas yells, his five-year-old form jumping to emphasize his point.

"*Yeeah*, Ma!" Seán, his twin, peeps up before laughing and hugging his mother.

"Oh, for the life of me I will *never* get

used to a summer Christmas," Imogen mumbles. She kisses the top of Seán's head, which prompts the other two boys to come and give her hugs too. She laughs and gives them all kisses. "All right, let's get going then, my darlings."

I take that as my cue to walk up to her. I pull her into my arms and take a deep breath, inhaling the scent of her. Even after over a decade together, her smell still drives me crazy. I'm so glad that I decided to move to Ireland all those years ago. I don't think I could have lived as full of a life without her. But once we found out that she was pregnant with the twins, we decided that we would move our growing family unit to Australia—plus, it was time to open up a second office for Tru Blu in Sydney. So with Sam overseeing the Asia branch in Tokyo, that just left me to sort out things here. Business is crazy good.

It was an effort, but we've moved to Bondi in Sydney, and it was the best decision we could have ever made. The kids absolutely love being able to go to the beach almost every single day—as long as they finish their homework, of course. The Australian coast was something I definitely took for granted when I was growing up, and I had definitely missed it while we were still living in Ireland. Sure, Ireland does have their own beaches, but nothing like the beaches we Aussies have. I didn't miss the heatwaves, though. They've been an absolute killer.

I begrudgingly release my wife with a kiss full on the lips, causing our boys to moan in disgust.

"*Ewwwww*, get a room, guys!" Ollie says, imitating his Aunt Riley perfectly.

"Yeah, get a room!" Seán and Thomas say in unison.

It's so strange having twins. And although the twins are at school now, we've still not gotten used to their unique qualities. They speak the same thing at the same time a lot, and they love to finish each other's sentences as if their minds really are linked up somehow. They *do* try to trick us into thinking they are the other twin, but we never fall for it—but their teachers do. They know exactly when the other needs them, too. Once, Thomas had pricked his foot on a shell while we were at the beach, and Seán, who wasn't anywhere near his twin, had perked up from the sandcastle that he was building and immediately dragged me over to Thomas before the latter had even started crying.

I give Imogen a look, which she returns

then nods. We both slowly walk up to the boys. "Ma, Dad? What are you doi—ah!" But before Seán can finish asking his question, Imogen and I wrap the boys in our arms and shower them with kisses, causing them all to burst into giggles.

"All right, let's get going then, boys. To the car!" she finishes dramatically.

"To the car!" the boys cry in unison and then run out to the family wagon parked in the driveway.

Imogen gives me one last smack on the lips. "I'll catch you later at our usual, yeah?" she asks.

"I wouldn't miss it for the world. *Tá grá agam duit*, Imogen Robinson," I say, trying not to butcher her beloved language.

"*Tá grá agam duit*, Leo Robinson," she says with a big smile before squeezing my hand and heading off to drop the boys off at school.

I shut the door behind her and sigh. I'm still so damn in love with that woman, it's unbelievable. I kept being told that we were going to fizzle out because we jumped into everything so quickly, but they were all wrong and I'm glad that they were. We've only grown closer and stronger over the years, and we've both enjoyed our roles as partners and parents very much. The sex has only gotten better and better. I love the look of Imogen when she's pregnant with our children—glowing like the true angel that she is. One of these days, we would love to have a daughter, too.

I go back into our open kitchen and finish responding to emails. We both still work together at Tru Blu Marketing and have been hard at work trying to expand the company further. Next stop, the Americas—mainly the US and Canada. We're hoping to keep it going by passing it down to our children, and the expansion would definitely help solidify that dream. We're a jet-setting family, and our kids have the unreal experience of getting to grow up all around the world, and they thrive with every new experience they get. Back when I was a kid, I thought life would forever be a battle, but the fates have aligned, and now I'm gliding along on cloud nine, my wife, my kids, and my business all providing a life I'd only dreamed of before. And even if I could do it all again, I wouldn't change a single thing. Because right here, right now, my world is perfectly complete.

And with that thought, I shut my laptop, put on my favorite pair of sunnies, and head out to the beach to meet with the love of my life. My forever. Imogen.

THE END...*ISH*

Ready to jump into the next book of the Curves Just Wanna Have Fun Series? Get Sweet Ride here—>

ALSO BY MEGAN WADE

Novels

Standalones

Mine for the Holidays

Wrong/Wright Series

Wrong Car, Wright Guy

Wrong Room, Wright Girl

Wrong Place, Wright Time

The Curves of Wall St.

Wall St Jerk

Wall St. Rascal

Novellas

Hermits & Curves Series

Sunshine & the Recluse

Cocktails & Curves Series

Swipe for a Cosmo

Old Fashioned Sweetie

Dark & Stormy Darlin'

Cute as a Lemon Drop

Happy Curves Series

Sheets & Giggles

Quilts & Chuckles

Sweet Curves Series

Marshmallow

Pumpkin

Pop

Sugarplum

Cookie

Sucker

Taffy

Toffee Apple

Peaches & Cream

Cupcake

Cheesecake

Wedded Curves Series

Whoa! I married a Mountain Man!

Whoa! I married a Billionaire!

Whoa! I married the Pitcher!

Whoa! I Married a Rock Star!

Whoa! I Married a Biker!

Sugar Curves

Sugar Honey Ice Tea

Yikes on a Cracker

What the Hell-o Kitty-Kat

Horse's Ask

Holy Cannoli

Hells Bells & Taco Shells

Holy Frozen Snowcones

Son of a Nutcracker

Curves Just Wanna Have Fun

Half Baked

Deep, Deep Donuts

Unexpected Sweetheart

Drink it Down

Sweet Ride

The Not So Silent Night

Cillian

Collaborations

518 Hope Ave (Cherry Falls)

GET IN TOUCH WITH MEGAN WADE

Megan Wade is a simple girl who believes in love at first sight and soulmates. She's obsessed with happy endings and Hallmark is her favorite brand of everything. Each Megan Wade story carries her 'Sugar Promise' of Over the Top Romance, Alpha Heroes, Curvy Heroines, Low Drama, High Heat and a Guaranteed Happily Ever After. What could be better than that?

email: contact@meganwadebooks.com

Newsletter: Get a copy of Rowdy Prince FREE when you sign up and confirm: https://www.subscribepage.com/meganwade_freebie

Amazon follow: click 'follow' on

Amazon when the rating window pops up on your device so the kindle app will notify you of new releases.

Facebook: https://www.facebook.com/meganwadeauthor/

Sweeties group: https://www.facebook.com/groups/9592116544649073

Instagram: https://www.instagram.com/meganwadewrites/

Printed in Great Britain
by Amazon